KIDS' SPORTS STORIES

WRESTLING WINNERS

by Elliott Smith

illustrated by Sophie Eves

PICTURE WINDOW BOOKS
a capstone imprint

Published by Picture Window Books, an imprint of Capstone
1710 Roe Crest Drive, North Mankato, Minnesota 56003
capstonepub.com

Library of Congress Cataloging-in-Publication Data
Names: Smith, Elliott, 1976- author.
Title: Wrestling winners / by Elliott Smith.
Other titles: Kids' sports stories.
Description: North Mankato, Minnesota : Picture Window Books, an imprint of Capstone, [2022] | Series: Kids' sports stories | Includes bibliographical references. | Audience: Ages 5-7. | Audience: Grades K-1. | Summary: Josiah joins a wrestling club, but because he is smaller than the other kids, he gets teased. One of the team members, Pablo, offers to coach him, and shows him a move that takes advantage of Josiah's quickness. It could be the secret weapon the team needs.
Identifiers: LCCN 2021023369 (print) | LCCN 2021023370 (ebook) | ISBN 9781663959386 (hardcover) | ISBN 9781666331820 (paperback) | ISBN 9781666331837 (pdf)
Subjects: LCSH: Wrestling--Juvenile fiction. | Teamwork (Sports)--Juvenile fiction. | Self-confidence--Juvenile fiction. | Friendship--Juvenile fiction. | CYAC: Wrestling--Fiction. | Teamwork (Sports)--Fiction. | Size--Fiction.
Classification: LCC PZ7.1.S626 Wr 2022 (print) | LCC PZ7.1.S626 (ebook) |DDC [E]--dc23
LC record available at https://lccn.loc.gov/2021023369
LC ebook record available at https://lccn.loc.gov/2021023370

Editorial Credits
Editor: Carrie Sheely; Designer: Bobbie Nuytten; Media Researcher: Morgan Walters; Production Specialist: Laura Manthe

Printed and bound in the United States of America. PO4608

TABLE OF CONTENTS

Glossary

 **meet**—a competition where individual wrestlers or two wrestling teams wrestle against each other

 **pin**—earning a win by holding your opponent's shoulders down on the mat for a certain amount of time; in folkstyle wrestling, the time is two seconds

 **shoot**—a quick move where one wrestler thrusts toward the opponent

 squat—a strength exercise where you crouch down with your knees bent

 takedown—a wrestling move where you take your opponent to the mat and control him or her

Chapter 1

HIT THE MAT

Josiah walked through school and stopped at the bulletin board. He saw a poster that caught his eye. A wrestling team! He thought wrestling would be so much fun. He took one of the flyers and ran home.

Josiah burst through the door. "Mom, can you sign me up for the wrestling team?" he asked excitedly.

His mom looked at the flyer. "Okay, Josiah. You can put your energy to good use."

Josiah smiled. He pictured himself

getting **pins**. *SLAM! WHAM!*

Josiah was excited when he arrived at practice. He took a quick look at the other kids. His excitement disappeared. He was the smallest one there. Josiah wondered if he had made a mistake joining.

"Hello team, my name is Coach Dan," a man said. "Welcome to our first practice. We are going to work hard and learn a lot. Each wrestler competes as an individual, but we are also a team. Let's get started!"

The team did push-ups, sit-ups, and **squats**. Josiah had a hard time doing them. They practiced **shooting**.

Then they learned some wrestling moves.
Each wrestler had a chance to try the
moves. Josiah felt like he was doing well!

Later, he got matched up with Ian.
Josiah dropped down. He tried to grab
Ian's legs. But Ian slipped away and took
Josiah down.

Then Josiah got paired with Travis.
WHAP! Josiah got pinned before he knew it.

"Oh wow, you're easy to take down,"
Travis said. Some of the other wrestlers
laughed. "You're too small to be a good
wrestler."

Josiah quickly walked away so no one
could see the tears in his eyes.

Chapter 2

LEARNING THE MOVES

After practice, another boy walked up to Josiah. "I heard what your partner said to you. Don't worry about it," the boy said. "My name is Pablo. Maybe I can help you? I know it can be tough learning a new sport."

Josiah smiled. "That would be great! You don't think I'm too small to wrestle?"

"Of course not," Pablo said. "At **meets**, you will get paired up with kids who weigh about the same as you. And I saw how fast you are. That will help you!"

Each week after practice, Josiah went to Pablo's house. They did push-ups and sit-ups. They practiced moves on Pablo's mat. Pablo had many wrestling videos. He showed Josiah some of the exciting matches.

Josiah began to feel more confident.
But he still worried he wasn't good enough.
After the next practice, Coach Dan said,
"We have our first meet of the season next
week. Everyone will wrestle. Each match
win scores points for our team. The team
with the most points wins."

Josiah heard Travis whisper behind him. "Well, we can count on Josiah losing," he said to Ian.

After practice, Josiah and Pablo walked to Pablo's house. "No one on the team thinks I can win," Josiah said. "Maybe they're right."

"I think you can win," Pablo said. "And I've got the perfect move for you to use."

Pablo taught Josiah how to do a single leg **takedown**. Josiah was fast enough to slide in and grab Pablo's leg. He could then knock Pablo off-balance and bring him down.

"Yes!" Josiah shouted. "I'm going to use this at the meet."

Chapter 3
EARNING RESPECT

Josiah bubbled with excitement the morning of the meet. When he walked into the gym, Pablo was waiting. "You're going up against Byron," he said. "He's really good."

Josiah suddenly felt nervous. *Am I good enough to win?* Josiah wondered.

It turned out Josiah and Byron's match was the last one. Josiah's team led by four points. How Josiah did could mean a win or a loss for the team. If he got pinned, his team would lose.

Josiah stepped onto the mat. He looked at Pablo. His friend gave him a thumbs up.

The match started poorly. Byron quickly got two takedowns. The score was 4–0! In round two, Josiah scored two points. He reversed two holds that Byron put him in.

It was 4–2 heading into the third and last round. "Let's go, Josiah!" Pablo yelled. Josiah decided it was time. He shot, grabbed Byron's heel, and took him to the mat. Two points! It was tied. But Byron scored one point right before the clock ran out.

Josiah lost 5–4. He dropped his head. But all around him, the team cheered! Josiah didn't get pinned, so the other team didn't get enough points to win.

"Uh, hey, good job out there," Travis said. "The team is going to get ice cream to celebrate. Want to come?"

"Sure!" Josiah said. He felt proud as he ran to join his teammates.

WALL SIT

Josiah and Pablo do exercises to build leg strength. One exercise you can do to build leg strength is a wall sit. You can do this by yourself or with a friend. If you do it with a friend, see who can last the longest!

What You Need:
- an open space on a wall
- a stopwatch or timer

What You Do:
- Find an open space next to a wall. Put your back against the wall and pretend you are sitting in a chair.
- Keep your knees at a 90-degree angle.
- Start the timer as soon as you are in the full squat position.
- Hold your wall sit as long as you can.
- Record your time.
- Go again and try to beat your time or go against a friend and see who can hold the wall sit longer.

REPLAY IT!

Take another look at this illustration. As Josiah steps onto the mat to face Byron, how do think Josiah felt? Have you ever felt a lot of pressure to perform really well?

Imagine you are Josiah. Write an email to your grandparents telling them how you felt right before the match started. Then write about what it felt like to help the team win.

ABOUT THE AUTHOR

Elliott Smith is a former sports reporter who covered athletes in all sports from high school to the pros. He is one of the authors of the Natural Thrills series about extreme outdoor sports. In his spare time, he likes playing sports with his two children, going to the movies, and adding to his collection of Pittsburgh Steelers memorabilia.

ABOUT
THE ILLUSTRATOR

Sophie Eves is a British illustrator represented by Lemonade Illustration Agency. She has a huge passion for visual storytelling and particularly enjoys designing for animation and illustrated books. She enjoys pursuing new challenges and fits in personal projects between her client work. Sophie lives in England.